THIS BOOK
BELONGS TO

Owen

Mrs. Corcoran

SK ~ Dec. 2011

For Patrick Regan,
my favorite writer

MARY ENGELBREIT'S
A MERRY LITTLE CHRISTMAS

CELEBRATE FROM A TO Z

HarperCollinsPublishers

IS FOR ANGEL
ATOP A TALL TREE,
AGLOW WITH THE LIGHT of
WHAT CHRISTMAS SHOULD BE.

 IS FOR BOXES WITH
RIBBONS AND BOWS
AND BOOTS THAT WE WEAR
TO KEEP WARM IN THE SNOW.

IS FOR COOKIES
AND CANDIES AND CAKES
AND A CUP OF HOT COCOA
THAT GRANDMOTHER MAKES.

D IS FOR DOLLHOUSES, DUMP TRUCKS, AND DRUMS BUILT IN THE WORKSHOP BEFORE CHRISTMAS COMES.

 IS FOR ELVES, SO SPRIGHTLY AND SMALL. WHEN SANTA NEEDS HELP, THEY ANSWER THE CALL.

IS FOR FROST
ON A COLD WINTER DAY
WHEN SNOWFLAKES ARE FALLING
AND FRIENDS COME TO PLAY.

G IS A GINGERBREAD COTTAGE. HOW GRAND! THE BEST DECORATIONS ARE THOSE MADE BY HAND.

 IS FOR HOME AND THE HAPPY HEARTS THERE AND THE HOLIDAY HOOPLA WE ALL LOVE TO SHARE.

IS FOR ICE SKATES ON LAKES SMOOTH AS GLASS AND ICICLES HANGING FROM EACH HOUSE WE PASS.

J IS FOR "*JINGLE BELLS*" SUNG LOUD AND LONG.
WHAT FUN WE HAVE SINGING
THAT JOLLY OLD SONG!

K 'S

FOR KALEIDOSCOPE,
KITE, AND KAZOO.
OH, HOW I HOPE THAT
DEAR SANTA COMES THROUGH!

L IS FOR LETTERS TO SANTA'S ADDRESS

AS FRIENDLY REMINDERS OF WHAT WE'D LIKE BEST.

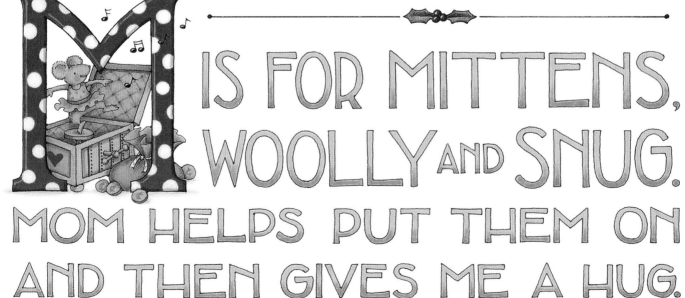

M IS FOR MITTENS, WOOLLY AND SNUG. MOM HELPS PUT THEM ON AND THEN GIVES ME A HUG.

IS THE NORTH POLE.
IT'S SANTA'S HOME BASE.
HIS GREAT JOLLY SMILE HELPS
TO WARM UP THE PLACE!

 IS FOR ORNAMENTS, FRAGILE AND OLD.
MOM SAYS THEY'RE PRICELESS, MORE PRECIOUS THAN GOLD.

 IS FOR PRESENTS
I WRAPPED BY MYSELF.
DAD SAYS, "REALLY GOOD!
LIKE THE WORK OF AN ELF."

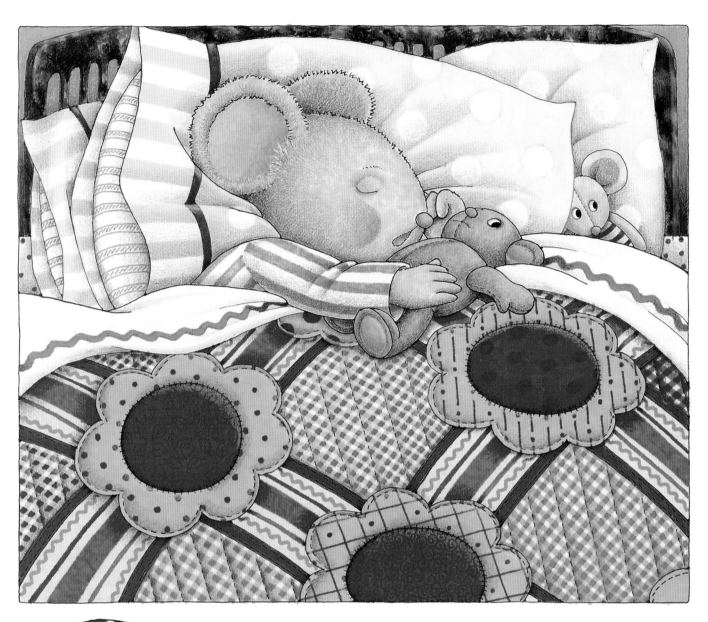

Q IS THE QUILT NESTLED UP TO MY CHIN
AS I DRIFT OFF TO SLEEP
UNTIL SANTA DROPS IN.

R IS FOR REINDEER THAT DASH THROUGH ᵗʰᵉ NIGHT AND LAND ON EACH ROOF ON A BLANKET OF WHITE.

IS FOR SLEIGH BELLS
SO MERRILY RINGING.
EACH JINGLE HOLDS PROMISE
OF WHAT SANTA'S BRINGING.

 IS FOR TINSEL
THAT HANGS FROM THE TREE
AND ALL THE TOYS SANTA
HAS LEFT THERE FOR ME.

U IS FOR UNCLES AND AUNTS AT THE DOOR, BRINGING KISSES AND COUSINS AND PRESENTS GALORE.

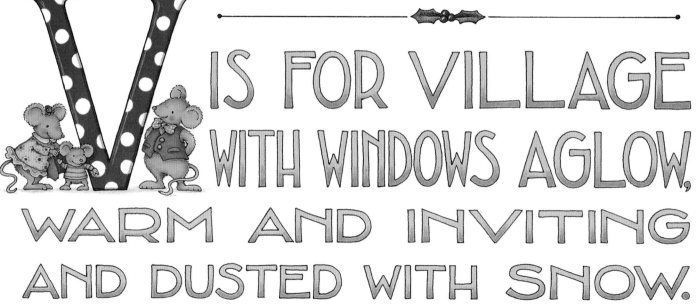

V IS FOR VILLAGE WITH WINDOWS AGLOW, WARM AND INVITING AND DUSTED WITH SNOW.

W IS FOR WREATHS ON WINDOWS AND DOORS, OUR WARM WAY OF WELCOMING THOSE WE ADORE.

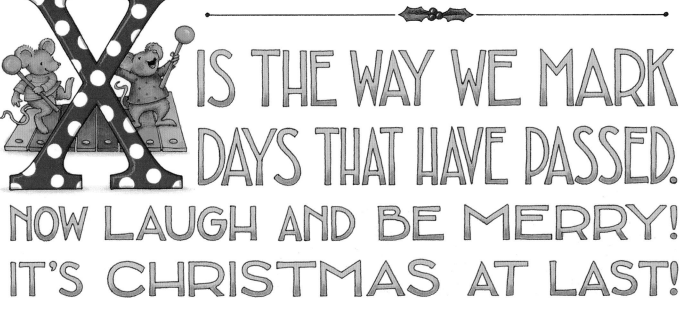

X IS THE WAY WE MARK DAYS THAT HAVE PASSED. NOW LAUGH AND BE MERRY! IT'S CHRISTMAS AT LAST!

 **Y** IS THE YULE LOG THAT GLOWS STRONG AND BRIGHT AS WE SHARE FAVORITE STORIES BY ITS WARM, DANCING LIGHT.

IS THE ZILLION WAYS
CHRISTMAS BRINGS CHEER.
MAY ITS MAGIC SHINE ON
EVERY DAY OF THE YEAR.

I would like to thank the staff at Mary Engelbreit
Studios who made this book possible, including
Pam Dobek, David Arnold, Wende Fink, Jackie
Ahlstrom, and Stephanie Barken.

❧

Mary Engelbreit's A Merry Little Christmas
Copyright © 2006 by Mary Engelbreit Ink

Manufactured in China.
All rights reserved. www.harpercollinschildrens.com

Library of Congress Cataloging-in-Publication
Data is available.
ISBN-10: 0-06-074158-9 — ISBN-13: 978-0-06-074158-7
ISBN-10: 0-06-074159-7 (lib. bdg.) —
ISBN-13: 978-0-06-074159-4 (lib. bdg.)

1 2 3 4 5 6 7 8 9 10
First Edition